GORDON LOGGINS

AND THE THREE BEARS

For Nico Lauck Stephenson and his big brother, Jeremie, and his little brother, Leo. — L.B.
For K.S. — T.W.

Text © 1997 Linda Bailey
Illustrations © 1997 Tracy Walker

Kids Can Press acknowledges the financial support of the Ontario Arts Council, the Canada Council for the Arts and the Government of Canada, through the BPIDP, for our publishing activity.

Published in Canada by
Kids Can Press Ltd.
29 Birch Avenue
Toronto, ON M4V 1E2

Published in the U.S. by
Kids Can Press Ltd.
2250 Military Road
Tonawanda, NY 14150

The artwork in this book was rendered in watercolor and ink.
The text is set in Sabon.

Edited by Debbie Rogosin and Trudee Romanek
Designed by Marie Bartholomew
Printed in Hong Kong by Wing King Tong Company Limited

The hardcover edition of this book is smyth sewn casebound.
The paperback edition of this book is limp sewn with a drawn-on cover.

CM 97 0 9 8 7 6 5 4 3 2 1
CM PA 01 0 9 8 7 6 5 4 3 2 1

Canadian Cataloguing in Publication Data

Bailey, Linda, 1948–
   Gordon Loggins and the three bears

ISBN 1-55074-362-7 (bound)   ISBN 1-55074-389-9 (pbk.)

I. Walker, Tracy. II. Title.

PS8553.A3644G67 1997   jC813'.54   C97-930197-1

PZ7.B34Go 1997

Kids Can Press is a Nelvana company

GORDON LOGGINS
AND THE THREE BEARS

WRITTEN BY LINDA BAILEY

ILLUSTRATED BY TRACY WALKER

KIDS CAN PRESS

Gordon Loggins couldn't believe his eyes. The books were moving. All by themselves.

He sat up straighter on the story-time carpet and looked again. Yes! A whole row of library books was slowly shifting to one side.

Gordon Loggins glanced around. His friend Zack had gone to the bathroom. The rest of the kids were giggling and wrestling. They were tired of waiting for the librarian to read them a story.

Gordon Loggins was the only one who had seen the books move.

He was the only one who saw the little door as it slowly, slowly opened. Inching closer, he peeked through the doorway.

There was a forest in there. Right there in the middle of the library! Gordon Loggins had gone on a tour of the library once. He'd seen the computer room and the coffee room and the room where they fixed books. Nobody had said a word about a forest.

In as much time as it takes to turn a page, Gordon Loggins darted through the doorway.

The trees were enormous. They rose so high that Gordon Loggins had to squint to see the ceiling. It was made of white tiles, just like the ceiling in the rest of the library.

Gordon Loggins only took a step or two. He only stared for a moment. But when he looked back, the door had vanished! All he could see was a path, leading to a little yellow house.

"Maybe it's an office," Gordon Loggins thought as he headed toward it.

No one answered when he knocked. Gordon Loggins lifted the latch and stepped inside. He noticed the bowls straight away. There were three — a great big bowl, a middle-sized bowl and a little wee bowl. Gordon Loggins walked over and stuck his finger into the middle-sized bowl.

"Ugh! Porridge." Gordon Loggins hated porridge more than anything. Especially this porridge. It was cold, and it had no sugar.

When a head peeked around the corner, Gordon Loggins nearly jumped out of his skin. The head was huge. And furry. And it wasn't alone. Two more furry bear heads peeked out, one small and one middle-sized.

"Who are you?" said the great huge bear in a deep, gruff voice.

"Gordon Loggins," said Gordon Loggins in a tiny, trembly voice.

"Did he say Goldilocks?" asked the middle-sized bear.

"It sounded like Goldilocks," squeaked the wee small bear.

The middle-sized bear marched up to Gordon Loggins and waggled a claw. "You're not Goldilocks," she growled. "Don't pretend that you are."

Gordon Loggins felt very much like crying. "I'm Gordon," he said. "Gordon Loggins."

"Golden Lockens?" The great huge bear lumbered in. "Never heard of you. Where's Goldilocks?"

"Maybe she's sick," said the middle-sized bear. "Maybe they sent *him* instead."

"Hmmph." The great huge bear circled Gordon Loggins slowly. "He's all wrong. He's too puny. And he hasn't got golden ringlets."

The middle-sized bear nodded. "You're right. He won't do at all."

Gordon Loggins gulped. "Won't do for what?"

"For the story, of course," said the wee small bear. "Goldilocks and the Three Bears. That's us. Papa Bear, Mama Bear and me — Baby Bear. But you're doing it wrong. You were supposed to taste *all* the bowls of porridge. You can't be in the story if you don't."

"I don't want to be in the story," said Gordon Loggins, his chin trembling. "I want to be back with the other kids."

"The kids!" said Mama Bear. "Listen. Can you hear them?"

Gordon Loggins held his breath. From far away, he could hear children's voices. "We want a story! We want a story!" Gordon Loggins thought he recognized the voice of his friend Zack.

"Where are they?" Gordon Loggins asked, looking around.

"Oh, we can't see them," said Baby Bear, "but they can see us. That's why we have to do the story right."

The chanting grew louder. "WE WANT A STORY!"

"Goodness gracious, dearie me." Mama Bear chewed nervously on a claw. "Well, he'll have to do. Come, young man, it's time to get started."

"But I'm not Goldilocks," Gordon Loggins protested.

"You can say that again," grumbled Papa Bear as he and Baby Bear disappeared around the corner.

"Don't worry, dear." Mama Bear gave Gordon Loggins a pat before waddling out. "We'll be right back here, explaining everything."

Gordon Loggins was left all by himself. The chanting had now become a huge roar. "WE WANT A STORY! WE WANT A STORY!"

Gordon Loggins took a step toward the table. Slowly the roar grew dimmer. He took a spoonful of porridge from the great big bowl, closed his eyes and — as fast as he could — swallowed.

"You're supposed to say it's too hot," hissed Baby Bear.

"I know," said Gordon Loggins. "I've heard this story." Looking around, he said in a loud voice, "This porridge is TOO HOT!"

"Good," whispered Mama Bear. "That was really good."

Gordon Loggins moved on to the middle-sized bowl, feeling quite proud of himself. He tasted a mouthful and said, "This porridge is TOO COLD!"

"Excellent!" said Papa Bear. "The boy's terrific."

A big grin spread across Gordon Loggins's face as he reached for the little wee bowl. Swallowing a spoonful, he pronounced in loud actor tones, "This porridge is JUST RIGHT!"

The three bears clapped. Gordon Loggins thought he could hear faint cheers from the story-time carpet. He grinned wider. Then he tried to remember what came next.

"You have to eat it all up," whispered Baby Bear.

Oh. Gordon Loggins had forgotten about this part. "I can't," he said.

Mama Bear's whisper came back. "Why not?"

"I hate porridge," said Gordon Loggins.

Three heads popped around the corner. "HATE PORRIDGE?" they boomed.

"You *must* eat it up," said Papa Bear.

"Think of the story-time children," said Mama Bear.

Gordon Loggins was racked with anguish. What to do? What to do? He didn't want to spoil story time. And he *did* want the story to end so he could get back to the carpet.

"Do you have any chocolate chips?" he asked.

A moment later, a paw poked around the corner. It was holding a bag of chocolate chips. Gordon Loggins sprinkled them on the porridge. They helped a lot. In a very short time, he had eaten up every bit.

"Now the chairs," whispered Baby Bear.

"I know," said Gordon Loggins. Looking around, he spotted three chairs. He headed for the great big one. He had to stretch his leg up very high to get onto it.

"This chair is TOO HARD!" he said.

Next he tried the middle-sized chair. It had a very oomphy cushion. "This chair is TOO SOFT!" said Gordon Loggins.

Finally, he went over to the little wee chair.

"This chair is JUST RIGHT!" he said as he sat down.

Gordon Loggins knew what was supposed to happen next. He waited. Nothing happened. He bounced up and down a couple of times.

"Hey, kid," whispered Papa Bear. "You're supposed to break the chair."

"I'm trying," Gordon Loggins hissed back. One, two, three more times, he jumped up and plopped down. Nothing.

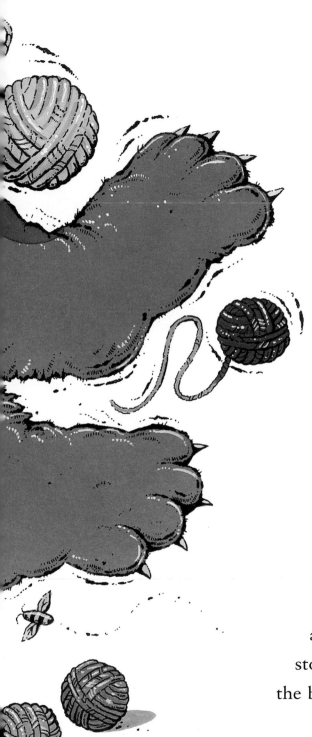

"Oh, for heaven's sake," said Papa Bear. In a great whoosh of brown fur, he came thundering into the room. Shoving Gordon Loggins aside, he leaped up and landed — CRASH — on the little wee chair. For just a second, he lay sprawled in the wreckage. Then, before Gordon Loggins could move, the huge bear scuttled out the door.

"I don't think anyone noticed," he whispered to Mama Bear. "Do you?"

"No, dear," replied Mama Bear. "I *told* you he was too puny."

"Am not puny," muttered Gordon Loggins. "And where's the bedroom around here anyway?" A paw came around the corner and pointed up.

Gordon Loggins was starting to get a bit tired of this story stuff. As he stomped up the stairs, he could hear the bears bumbling along behind him.

"I *know* what to do next," Gordon Loggins declared as he scrambled onto the great big bed. It was as hard as a slab of granite. "Ouch!" he said, rubbing his knees. "Too hard."

When he hopped onto the middle-sized bed, it sagged and collapsed all around him. "Oof! Way too soft," spluttered Gordon Loggins.

The little wee bed was covered with a thick, fluffy quilt. It was not too hard and not too soft, and it was exactly as long as Gordon Loggins.

Gordon Loggins yawned. He had had an extremely difficult morning. He lay down on the little bed and closed his eyes . . .

It was the whispering that woke him.

"He must have been terribly tired," murmured Mama Bear.

"I know," agreed Papa Bear, "but the children are waiting."

"All right," said Mama Bear. "Go ahead. Growl at him."

"Me?" said Papa Bear. "Why don't you growl at him?"

"We'll all growl at him," said Baby Bear. "But not too loudly. We don't want to scare him."

Gordon Loggins kept his eyes shut tight. He kept his body perfectly still. He could hear the three bears creeping closer. He could feel soft bear fur against his hand and a wet bear nose nuzzling his elbow. Gordon Loggins waited until the three bears were so close he could smell the porridge on their breath.

And *that's* when Gordon Loggins did it.

"GRRROWWRRRR!" roared Gordon Loggins, leaping straight up in the air.

And one more time, even louder, "GRRROWWRRRR!"

The three bears flew backward. Their claws scrabbled against the floor as they tried to get away. They tumbled all over top and underneath one another in a mixed-up, wrassling, somersaulting, scrambling heap of brown flying fur on the floor.

"Yip, yip, squeeee!" went the three bears. "Iyy, oww, wee, wee, weeeeee!"

The first one to stop thrashing
was Papa Bear. He started to laugh.
Mama Bear laughed, too. Then Baby
Bear joined in. The three bears
laughed so hard the house shook.
Gordon Loggins laughed with them.

When he finally stopped to catch his breath, he was sure he
could hear the kids back at story time. They were roaring with
laughter. The loudest of all was Zack.

"What a guy," said Papa Bear with a final chuckle. "What do
you think, Mama? This Golden Lockens is a pretty funny kid."

"It's *Gordon*," said Gordon Loggins as politely as he could.
"Can I go back now?"

"Of course," said Papa Bear. "You only had to ask."

The three bears led Gordon Loggins outside and back down
the path. There — just like magic — was the tiny door.

Gordon Loggins said good-bye to the three bears and shook
their paws. He even thanked them for the porridge. Then he
scuttled through the doorway faster than a book closing.

Back on the other side, the library looked exactly the way a library is supposed to look. Gordon Loggins was very happy to see the story-time carpet again, and the books, and the kids, and the librarian. He was especially happy to see his friend Zack.

"Hey, Gordon," said Zack. "Where've you been? You missed a great story. Golden Lockens and the Three Bears."

"It's not Golden Lockens," said Gordon Loggins. "It's —"

Gordon Loggins stopped. He stared hard at the book in Zack's hand. There they were — Mama Bear, Papa Bear and Baby Bear. And there he was, too. Gordon Loggins! He was sure that boy was him, even if he did look a bit puny.

"Can I read it?" asked Gordon Loggins.

As Gordon Loggins opened the book, he heard a sound that made him smile. Maybe it was just the crackle of pages turning. Or maybe it was a sound he had heard not very long before.

The sound of three bears clapping.